Disney · PIXAR
Merida

The Ghostly Horse

To Anika —S.B.Q.

randomhousekids.com

ISBN 978-0-7364-3515-4 (hc)

Printed in the United States of America

10 9 8 7 6 5 4 3 2 1

DISNEY · PIXAR

Merida

The Ghostly Horse

By Sudipta Bardhan-Quallen
Illustrated by Gurihiru

Random House 🏠 New York

Chapter 1

Merida looked at her father, King Fergus of
DunBroch. He wrung his hands in despair. "I just
don't know," Fergus said. "I can't imagine how
this is going to work."

"Oh, Dad." Merida sighed. "You've got to
calm down. We'll figure it out."

"It's impossible! Hopeless!" Fergus bellowed.

"There's only so much a man can do, even if he is the king!" He threw his arms up in the air. "There's no way I can fit all this stuff into just one wagon!"

The look of anger and frustration on Fergus's face made Merida finally crack. She giggled, quietly at first, but it progressed into a full-bellied laugh. Fergus scowled for a moment longer. But then he laughed, too.

"Here, lass," Fergus said, tossing Merida a small bundle. "Cram that in somewhere."

It was small enough for Merida to tuck into one of Angus's saddlebags. He whinnied and she patted his nose. "Don't worry, boy," she whispered. "I won't load you up too much."

Turning back to her father, Merida said, "We're going to need another wagon, Dad.

Especially if Mum insists on bringing three bags of shoes."

"We're going to our cabin at the loch for one week," Fergus grumbled, though his eyes were sparkling. "How many shoes can she wear? She only has the one set of feet!"

"Don't let Mum hear you say that," Merida warned.

"Too late for that." Queen Elinor's voice came from behind them.

Merida and Fergus glanced at each other before they faced the queen. Merida bit her lip and smiled, while Fergus shrugged. "Sorry, love. I know you need every last pair of these shoes."

Elinor arched an eyebrow and looked coldly at her husband and daughter. Then she grinned. "A woman must be prepared for anything," she said, removing a pair of fancy embroidered slippers from one of her bags. "What if we have guests at the loch?"

Fergus snorted. "Yes, dear. Maybe we'll need to host a dinner party at our secluded, private royal cabin—where all visitors are prohibited. The only guest we're likely to have is Martin when he rides out to give us our daily update on DunBroch. And he doesn't care about slippers." He riffled through the bag as well and came out with a pair of sturdy brown boots. "And what are these for? Are you planning to hike through the marshes?"

Elinor snatched the boots from her husband. "What if I'm being chased by a kelpie?" she asked. "I'll need these to get away. Merida, make sure you are prepared as well."

"Why not warn her against a dancing, charging bubu, or a giant?" Fergus muttered.

Elinor turned to her daughter. "After everything this family has been through, your father still doesn't believe in magic."

"Magic, yes," Fergus said. "Bubus and kelpies, no. Those are just tales parents tell their children when they want to scare them into behaving."

"You're wrong, Dad," Merida said. "Kelpies are dangerous. They've drawn hundreds of sailors to their doom with their mesmerizing songs."

"I think that's mermaids," Fergus quipped.

"Oh," Merida said. "Then kelpies have incinerated entire villages with their fiery breath."

"That's dragons," Fergus said.

Merida couldn't hold back any longer. She

covered her mouth with her hand and giggled. Even Angus seemed to nicker at the joke. Elinor shrugged. "For the record," she said, "kelpies are half human and half horse, and it is well known that they kidnap children and drown them."

"I know, dear," Fergus said. "I promise that if we see any men with horse tails poking out of their kilts, we will run away as fast as we can."

Elinor frowned and tucked her boots back into her bag. "It is better to be ready than not."

Fergus chuckled.

"And speaking of being ready, Mum," Merida said, "should I go fetch the boys so we can leave?"

Elinor nodded. "A fine idea, lass. I'll come with you."

"Just don't bring back anything but the lads and their *very wee* bags," Fergus grumbled, still trying to shove bundles onto the overstuffed wagon.

Merida and Elinor walked in step as they made their way toward the Great Hall of Castle DunBroch. For a few moments, they were silent. Then Merida said, "I'm glad we're taking this trip. It will be nice for all of us to spend some time together."

Elinor put an arm around her daughter's shoulders. "I love the cabin by the loch. Even though it's less than a morning's ride away, it feels like a different world. It's always so peaceful there." She grinned. "Except for the kelpies, of course."

Merida giggled. Then she glanced at her mother out of the corner of her eye. "You know what would make it more peaceful? If we left the triplets at DunBroch with Maudie."

Elinor laughed. "It's hardly a family vacation if we don't bring the whole family."

"I suppose," Merida sighed. "It's just that they're always getting into trouble!"

"I know, lass," Elinor said. "But I remember a wee girl who was always getting into trouble at their age as well." Mother and daughter smiled at each other. Then Elinor added, "And actually, she still finds herself in a dilemma now and then."

"Oh, Mum," Merida groaned. "It's different when it's me!"

"It always is," Elinor said.

They entered the hall. Merida scanned the room for Harris, Hubert, and Hamish. She knew if she found one brother, she'd find all three. And she was right. Someone had left a plate of sweetcakes unattended on a table. As Merida looked on, three hands poked up from under the table. In a flash, the plate was gone and she heard the distinctive sounds of three wee lads stuffing their gobs.

"See what I mean, Mum?" Merida pointed. "I never did *that.*"

"Boys!" Elinor shouted, lifting the tablecloth to reveal her sons. "Come out at once!" Elinor's eyes narrowed as she stared down each of her sons individually. "The last time you boys did something like this, you had dreadful collywobbles for days! What have you got to say for yourselves?"

The triplets glanced at one another. Hamish shrugged. Hubert scratched his head. Harris gazed down at his toes.

Merida rolled her eyes. Her brothers would never change.

"I'm going to the kitchen to pack some gingerroot tea, in case you three need it later to settle your tummies," Elinor said. "You lads go on and finish packing your bags."

When Elinor had left, Merida addressed the triplets. "Come on, lads. Get your bags so we can go when Mum is ready. I'll wait for you outside."

The boys nodded. They knew what to do. They gestured to their sister that they'd be right back and then scurried off.

Merida walked into the sunlight, listening to the sounds of the bustling castle. It would be nice to be far away from all that commotion for a few days. Best of all, at the cabin she didn't have to be Princess Merida, who was burdened with all sorts of lessons, responsibilities, and obligations. There she was just Merida, a girl with nothing to worry about except how long to ride or how much fish to eat.

Merida was lost in thought. When Harris tapped her arm, she was startled. "You're back already?" The boys nodded innocently, holding their bags.

Merida cocked her head. What were they up to? They appeared to be cooperating—but Merida never knew what to expect with them. Still, there didn't seem to be anything obviously suspicious. So with one last big-sisterly look, Merida led the triplets away. "Let's find Dad," she said.

Soon the boys were running in front of her,

straight for the gatehouse, where their dad was waiting with the wagon. He was still struggling with getting every last bundle packed away. He spied his children and a huge grin broke across his face.

"Lads! Merida!" Fergus bellowed. "Are we ready to leave for the loch?"

The triplets looked sideways at one another and grinned before nodding.

"I'll try to fit your bags onto the wagon, then," Fergus said. When the boys hurried away, he turned to Merida. "Where's your mother? Please don't tell me she's packing more bags."

Merida shook her head. "Mum's getting some tea for the boys," she told him. "She said we should finish loading the wagon."

"Easy for her to say," Fergus griped. He took a

bundle off the wagon and handed it to Merida. "Can you put this in Angus's saddlebag? I need to rearrange some things."

Fergus leaned into the wagon to try and move some bundles around. He wasn't looking at the triplets. But Merida and Angus saw them.

Hamish and Hubert opened their bags. They each carefully took a small mouse from inside. "Hamish! Hubert! No!" Merida yelled. But the

boys just smirked at her. Then they snuck up behind Fergus and dropped their mice down the back of his kilt.

"Jings crivens help ma boab!" Fergus yelped. "What was that?" The mice darted around under the fabric of the kilt. When Fergus realized what was crawling on him, he cried, "Is someone playing a joke on me?" He grabbed at the mice. But all that his flailing accomplished was to fling bags right and left.

Merida rushed to help her father. "Here, let me. . . ." But she wasn't fast enough to catch the mice either.

To make matters worse, Harris opened the bag he'd been carrying. Out came a small calico cat. Almost immediately, the cat caught the scent of the mice and jumped onto poor

Fergus. And then Fergus's yelps were joined by squeaking, hissing, and the plops of bags falling off the wagon.

"What in the world is going on?" Elinor's voice cut through the commotion.

Immediately, the triplets froze and Fergus stopped yelping. Even the cat and the mice seemed to slow down.

"Do you want to go to the loch or not?" Elinor asked. Her entire family nodded. "Then you'd better get this wagon packed before I change my mind about whether you all *deserve* a holiday!"

That sent Fergus and the triplets scurrying to gather the fallen bags and get them back on the wagon. Merida, too, would have been repacking, but Elinor stopped her. She drew her daughter aside. "Merida," she said, "those boys of mine—all *four* of them—are a handful. You're the one I trust to be responsible when I'm not around."

"This wasn't my fault!" Merida said.

Elinor held a finger to Merida's lips to shush her. "I know, lass. You won't be able to stop their foolishness a lot of the time. I just want you to know that you have my permission to take care of them—and be firm when needed—if I'm not here."

Merida sighed. Another responsibility.

As if she could read her daughter's mind, Queen Elinor patted Merida's cheek. "Don't worry, Merida. We'll be together all through our holiday. So this is a responsibility you won't have to worry about for a while."

Chapter 2

The boys of Clan DunBroch repacked the wagon as fast as they could. Soon the family was on the road to the cabin. Merida and Elinor rode their horses, while Fergus drove the wagon holding the bags and the triplets. The only sounds were the clopping of horse hooves, Mum's soft humming, and Dad's whistling. It was a peaceful ride, and Merida felt herself relaxing.

They arrived at the cabin hungry. "Let's eat before we unpack," Elinor decided. She got no complaints from anyone.

The family set up their picnic. Merida ate a meat pie and then lay back in the grass. Mum and Dad sat next to each other holding hands, watching their sons stuff their gobs—right until Hamish tossed an apple and hit Fergus in the belly with it. Fergus roared with laughter and went off in pursuit of the boys. Soon the four were happily chasing one another in the open field in front of the cabin.

Mum came over and sat next to Merida. Together, they gazed lazily out at the loch. Every once in a while, a fish would leap out of the water, its scales glistening in the sun.

Elinor spied a family of deer having a drink at the water's edge. "Look, Merida," she whispered, pointing.

Merida looked at the deer. "They're on a family holiday, too." She laughed.

Then she saw something else. Just beyond the deer family, another animal stood on the banks of the loch. But it was all white and wearing a bridle, so it couldn't be a deer. "Mum,

is that a horse over there?" Merida asked.

Elinor strained to see. "It seems to be. But there are no wild horses in these parts."

Merida wanted to find out more about the animal. But when she rose to get a better look, something else caught her eye. Two strangers were riding in the direction of the cabin, one of them holding a Clan DunBroch banner. "Mum!" she gasped. "Look!"

Elinor turned toward the riders. "One is clearly a DunBroch guard. But the other rider is wearing MacGuffin colors. We weren't expecting to hear from Clan MacGuffin."

Merida glanced back at the loch. The approaching riders had scared away the deer family—and the horse.

The riders dismounted. Merida recognized

the guard as Gordon. He approached Elinor. "Pardon me, My Queen," he said, "but I believe you and the king are needed."

Elinor nodded. She stood up and brushed at her skirts.

"Is everything all right, Mum?" Merida asked.

"I hope so," Elinor answered. But she was frowning. "Go fetch your father, please."

Merida gulped. If there was a problem with the clans, Elinor would consider it her duty to help. And that would mean their holiday was in peril.

As she walked to get her father, Merida looked back at Mum and the MacGuffin rider. They were deep in conversation, but too far away for Merida to hear what they were saying.

At least Elinor still appeared calm—if Mum's face showed panic, Merida would have been a lot more worried.

"Dad," Merida said, "Mum needs you."

"What's going on?" Fergus asked. "Did I forget to pack some of her shoes?"

Merida shook her head. "A rider came from Clan MacGuffin," she said.

"Clan MacGuffin?" Fergus scratched his head. "Why would they send a rider?"

Merida shrugged. "Let's go find out."

By the time Merida and Fergus got to Elinor, the conversation was over. The riders were watering their horses, clearly preparing to head out again. But from the look on Mum's face, Merida knew the news wasn't good.

"Fergus, Merida, I'm glad you're here,"

Elinor said. "I've just received word from Lord MacGuffin that there is a dispute in his clan that is causing a great ruckus. Something about a barrel of potatoes . . . At any rate, the dispute has gotten so out of hand that it requires royal help to settle."

"No!" Fergus shouted. "Don't make me go to MacGuffin lands. I don't understand the people there at all!"

"I know their traditions may be different from ours—" Elinor began.

Fergus interrupted her. "Traditions? I'm talking about that accent!" He leaned closer to whisper in Merida's ear. "I barely understand a word they say."

Merida giggled. Even Elinor couldn't hide her amusement.

"Lucky for you, Husband," Elinor said, "they specifically asked that the queen come to settle the dispute. They obviously realize I'm the more diplomatic ruler in this family. So all you have to do is accompany me."

"But we just got here!" Merida exclaimed. Her cry got the attention of the triplets, who came over to see what was going on.

"Aye!" cried Fergus. "You don't have time to ride a whole day to settle potato disputes or MacGuffin silliness. We are on holiday!"

Elinor shook her head. "I'm afraid I cannot stay. I have a responsibility to my people. When they ask for help, I must be there to assist them." She gave her family a weak smile. "It won't take long," she added. "One day there, one day to talk, one day back."

No one in the family returned Elinor's smile. She studied each of them and then turned to Fergus. "We can leave some of the shoes here," she offered. But Fergus just sighed.

Merida looked away and traced the toe of her shoe along the dirt. It wasn't fair that they *all* had to give up their holiday. Then she had an idea. "Why don't I stay here with Dad," she suggested. "You can take the triplets with you to help the MacGuffins."

Harris, Hubert, and Hamish crossed their arms, unhappy with Merida's suggestion. But Fergus grinned. "A fine idea, lassie! But there's no reason for your mum to take the lads. I'll take care of you all!"

This time, the triplets agreed, nodding enthusiastically. Merida thought that might be pushing it—but at least it would keep her at the loch.

They all looked at Elinor. But she was frowning and shaking her head. "I can't let you stay here without me," she said. "Remember the chaos you got into back at DunBroch when I was just a few moments away?"

Fergus and the boys hung their heads. But Merida stepped forward. "I remember what happened. But you asked me to take care of these galoots if you aren't around. Now I'm asking you to trust me to do that."

Elinor gazed at her daughter and bit her lip. Fergus noticed his wife weakening, so he added his appeal. He put his hands on Elinor's arms and smiled. "Come on, dear. We can handle a few days. Like you said, one day there, one day for you to work your magic, and one day back."

"Please, Mum?" said Merida.

Even the triplets begged with their hands clasped.

For a moment, Elinor said nothing. Then she threw her hands in the air. "All right, all right. I give up! I'll go deal with the MacGuffins alone and come back here as soon as I can."

Merida and the boys cheered, and Fergus lifted Elinor off the ground. She giggled, then tapped his shoulder, asking to be let down. She took a few bags off the wagon and put them in her horse's saddlebags. "Please get all this unpacked while I'm gone," she said, mounting her horse. "I'll leave right away."

Merida, Fergus, and the triplets waved and called out their good-byes as Elinor rode off.

"Stay out of trouble. Merida, you're in charge!"

"Huh?" Fergus said, confused. But Merida just elbowed him in the ribs and kept waving.

"And don't be abducted by a kelpie!" Elinor shouted.

"Stop worrying, Mum!" Merida answered. "How much trouble can we get into on holiday?"

Chapter 3

It took most of the day after Elinor's departure to unpack their possessions. The sky grew dark as Fergus put away the last of the bags.

"Did your mother take *anything* with her?" Fergus complained.

Merida giggled. "I thought I saw her take

two bags of shoes!" she told her father.

"Clearly, I was wrong about magic earlier," Fergus grumbled. "There must be some wicked force at this loch that makes luggage multiply when we're not looking." He shook his head. "I think I've finally gotten everything. Can you go check Angus's saddlebags to make sure nothing's been left there?"

"Of course, Dad." Merida gave her father a kiss on the cheek. "I'll even keep my eye out for that wicked magic," she joked.

She could hear Fergus's colorful complaining all the way to the paddock. There was nothing in Angus's saddlebags, so she yelled, "All clear here, Dad!"

Merida nuzzled her horse's nose as the two of them gazed out at the moonlit water. "Isn't it beautiful, Angus?" she asked.

Angus whinnied.

"This is going to be a wonderful trip," Fergus called from the cabin. "We'll have gobs of fun with nothing and no one to bother us!"

Merida gave Angus an apple and brushed his coat gently. "It was a long ride, wasn't it, boy? You must be tired. I bet you're glad we're staying here and not traveling to the MacGuffin lands."

Angus swished his tail happily.

"I'm glad we're staying, too," Merida said. "Tomorrow we'll go for a relaxing ride around the loch. Maybe Dad will join us!"

Fergus appeared in the doorway. "Sounds lovely, lass," he said, looking around the yard. "Merida, have you seen the boys?"

Merida shrugged. "Aren't they in the cabin?

I thought they'd be there helping you."

"Ha!" Fergus grunted. "As if those lads have ever helped me with anything."

Merida laughed. Dad was right. Still, it was strange for the triplets not to be underfoot. "Angus and I will look around for them."

Merida rode back and forth along the shore of the loch in front of the cabin. But she didn't see any red curly hair or freckled faces.

"Where could they be, Angus?" Merida asked. "They're on foot—they can't have gone far."

She decided to ride farther down the shore. Only after the cabin was far behind them did she and Angus spy the boys. "How did they get all the way here?" Merida wondered.

The triplets were heading to the loch. They

looked as if they were in a trance. The three boys moved steadily, without paying attention to anything around them. "If they wanted a nighttime swim, why go so far from the cabin?" Merida asked.

Angus snorted. He sped up to reach the boys faster.

When they got a bit closer, Merida realized

that it wasn't the water or the thought of a nighttime swim that had her brothers entranced. It had to be the beautiful white horse standing on the water's edge.

"Angus, look at that," Merida whispered, pointing. "I knew I'd seen a horse earlier!"

The horse must have just stepped out of the loch. She was still dripping water from her mane and tail. Merida could tell she wasn't wild because she wore a delicate silver bridle. "I wonder where her owner is," she said.

The horse tossed her head and looked over her shoulder. That was when Merida saw her stunning green eyes. She didn't understand it, but the more she stared at the horse, the more she wanted to reach her. Maybe even to ride her.

"Do you want to go meet her, Angus?" Merida asked. But before she could urge him toward the loch, Angus lurched forward. "Whoa, boy!" she commanded. But Angus didn't listen.

The triplets approached the white horse slowly, as if they didn't want to spook her. Angus, on the other hand, didn't seem to care. He galloped full speed directly at the horse, despite Merida's attempts to slow him down.

"Angus!" she hollered. "What are you doing?" It was almost as if he'd decided that he didn't like the other horse based solely on the first glance.

The white horse heard Angus's hoofbeats as he raced toward her. She stared for a moment and then reared up and neighed. The lads had almost reached her, but they weren't scared.

They kept walking at the same steady pace.

Angus didn't slow down either. If anything, he seemed to run faster.

The white horse must have sensed that Angus wanted a confrontation. She spun around and raced off before the triplets or Angus reached her.

When the horse was gone, Angus slowed. "Were you trying to drive her away?" Merida asked. She jumped from the saddle and positioned herself to look in Angus's eyes. "Were you jealous, boy?"

Angus tossed his head, and his tail swished hard and fast. He seemed more angry than jealous. Merida didn't know what to think.

When she looked at her brothers, they appeared to be coming out of a daze. They were probably surprised by Angus's behavior, just as she was. Merida called out to the triplets, "How did you three get this far from the cabin? Did you follow that horse all the way here?"

The three boys shrugged.

What a strange night, Merida thought, shaking her head. "Dad wants you back at the cabin," she said. "Let's go."

As they made their way home, Merida couldn't stop thinking about Angus chasing the other horse off.

Chapter
4

Merida almost never woke up early. But watching the sun rise over the loch was too brilliant a sight to miss. And with her brothers too young to appreciate such a sunrise, she got to spend the time alone with her father.

"Your mother also loves sunrises," Fergus said.

"Do you think she'll be back even sooner than she said?" Merida asked.

"I doubt it." Fergus chuckled. "I know your mother thought it would only take a day, but a MacGuffin potato dispute probably takes two days to resolve. The day after tomorrow is more likely."

Merida groaned. She missed Mum—a family holiday just wasn't the same without the whole family. But maybe this was a chance to have some time alone with her father. "Can we go for a ride today, Dad? Just you and me?"

Fergus shook his head. "Who would watch the boys?"

Merida frowned. "Can't they stay by themselves for a while?"

Dad laughed. "We promised your mother

there wouldn't be any trouble while she was gone. I'm keeping an eye on those boys all day long. In fact, I'm going to wake them up and start this day off on the right foot!" He stood and began to walk toward the cabin, then turned back to Merida. "I'm sorry, lass. When your mother returns, we'll take that ride. For now, why don't you go with Angus?"

Merida sighed. It wasn't the same as going with Dad, but Angus was wonderful company, too. She went to the stable and led Angus out to the field in front of the cabin, where Fergus had set up a large trough to water the family's horses. "Good morning, boy," she said. She brushed his coat and Angus swatted his tail lazily, enjoying the attention.

Suddenly, Angus's whole body went stiff.

Then he tossed his head and pawed at the ground. Merida stopped brushing. "Did I hurt you?" she asked.

When Angus didn't calm down, Merida followed his gaze to see what was upsetting him. She saw a woman walking toward the royal cabin.

Yesterday, two riders had arrived at the loch unannounced. Today, it was a stranger. Merida couldn't remember this much company during any of their holidays. "Dad!" she shouted. "Someone is coming!"

Angus kept snorting at the woman, so Merida stroked his muzzle to calm him. She also studied the woman who approached them.

The woman was beautiful. She was tall, with long, silvery-gold hair. She didn't wear it pulled

back like Mum. Instead, her hair was loose, and had clearly been recently washed—the ends were dripping. Her dress was blue, the same shade as the loch. It looked like no dress Merida had ever seen. The sleeves and the skirt were full, but the material was so fine that the fabric appeared to be flowing, glistening water. A long silver necklace glittered at her throat.

By the time the woman reached Merida and Angus, Fergus and the triplets had come out of the cabin. Fergus greeted the stranger.

"Hello, my lady," he said. "Can I help you?"

"I saw that there was someone here," the woman replied. "I wanted to come and say hello. My name is Eachna. I'm pleased to meet you."

Angus tensed once again. "Boys," Merida

whispered to her brothers as she stepped toward her father, "can you stay with Angus? He's anxious and I don't want him to be alone."

The triplets nodded.

"I'm Fergus of Clan DunBroch," Fergus answered. "These are my children, Merida, Hamish, Harris, and Hubert." He pointed to each of them in turn.

"How lovely!" Eachna beamed. "Your children are just darling!"

When Eachna laughed, Merida noticed one flaw in her otherwise perfectly beautiful face. She curled her upper lip as she laughed, showing her teeth—which were a wee bit too large.

Almost immediately, Merida felt bad for having such a mean thought. Eachna was just trying to be friendly. Merida knew Mum would expect her to be as gracious and welcoming as a princess should be.

"Thank you, Lady Eachna," Merida said. She signaled to her brothers to smile at their visitor as well.

"We weren't expecting company. Do you live nearby, Lady Eachna?" Fergus asked.

"Yes, just past that hill," Eachna replied.

Merida raised an eyebrow. "I didn't think there were any other houses near here," she said. "The royal cabin was built to give us privacy and safety."

"Royal—royal cabin?" Eachna stammered. "Does that mean . . . you're *King* Fergus?"

Dad nodded and grinned.

"I'm so sorry. I didn't know this was a royal cabin," Eachna continued. She smiled again, but this time her green eyes narrowed a bit. "When I arrived at the loch, there was no one here. I built my small house thinking I was free to do so. How could I have known this land belonged to the King of DunBroch?"

"Um, maybe because of the banners with the DunBroch sword hanging everywhere?" Merida said.

"However it happened, we're pleased to meet you," Fergus said. He shot Merida a look: *Remember your manners.*

Merida rolled her eyes but forced herself to obey her father's request.

"Thank you, King Fergus. You are too kind,"

Eachna said. Her gratitude was so exaggerated that for a moment, Merida wondered if she was faking it. But why would she? Merida tried to shake off the feeling. Dad had just reminded her to be polite, so Merida turned away to hide the doubt on her face.

That was when she saw how the triplets had calmed Angus down.

Her horse had dropped onto the field and was rolling over and over in a patch of mud. He was having so much fun that the boys had joined in. All four were now coated in mud— and showed no signs of stopping!

"Angus!" Merida shrieked. "Harris! Hamish! Hubert! Stop that at once!"

Fergus and Eachna turned to see what the

fuss was about. When Dad saw his mud-covered sons, his jaw dropped. "Boys! What are you doing?" He rushed over to the triplets. "You're filthy! What would Mum say if she saw you like this?"

Chapter 5

Harris, Hamish, Hubert, and Angus all hung their heads and shuffled left and right. Merida had to clamp her hand over her mouth to keep from cackling with glee. She knew why Dad was upset—but she also thought the whole situation was hilarious.

It was Eachna who finally broke the silence.

"King Fergus," she said, "may I offer some assistance? It would be my pleasure to take your sons for a swim in the loch to get them clean and free of mud." She smiled that same toothy smile once again.

"I think that would be all right," Fergus answered. "Merida, what do you think?"

Merida beamed. If Eachna was watching the boys, not only could she go riding with Dad, but Eachna would be the one stuck getting the triplets clean. And Merida knew from experience how hard that could be!

Both Fergus and Eachna read the look on Merida's face as a sign of agreement. "Go on ahead, boys," Fergus said. "Just try not to get our new friend wet."

"Don't worry." Eachna laughed. "I don't mind

the water at all. Go get your horse so you and the princess can have a break."

Fergus bowed and said, "Thank you for your help, my lady." He turned to Merida. "Maybe you should get Angus to the loch to get him cleaned up. Then we can head out."

Merida nodded.

As Fergus walked away, Merida went to Angus. "Come on, boy," she urged. But Angus stubbornly stood his ground.

At the same time, Eachna approached the triplets. "Hamish," she said, "come take my right hand, and Harris, you take my left. Hubert, you can lead the way to the water." Eachna held out her hands.

But like Angus, the boys refused to move—

apart from crossing their arms and raising their chins stubbornly. Merida knew why, even if Eachna didn't.

"Hamish! Harris! Hubert! Didn't you hear me?" Eachna's voice had an edge to it now. The boys still didn't move.

"Um, Lady Eachna," Merida piped up, "I think

you mean Hubert, Hamish, and Harris, don't you?" Merida pointed to the correct brother as she said each name. The triplets grinned three muddy grins at her for a moment, then went back to glowering at Eachna.

Eachna smiled at Merida, but the smile didn't reach her eyes. "I apologize for my mistake," she said, her voice suddenly colder. She stared at the boys and said, "Come along, lads. Your father wants you to accompany me."

Even though Merida had been eager to see the triplets go with Eachna just a few moments ago, she felt uneasy about that plan now. On instinct, she stepped between Eachna and her brothers. Angus followed, and Merida noticed that he still seemed tense.

Eachna didn't even bother to smile this time. She glared at Merida and Angus and said, "You should keep your distance, Princess Merida. You don't want to get any mud on you." She was about to walk around Merida when Angus squealed. The sound startled Eachna and she stumbled back a few steps.

Suddenly, Angus rushed to the boys and nudged them with his muzzle. The triplets jumped onto his back, and in a moment, Angus and the boys were galloping away.

"Angus!" Merida yelled. "Where are you going?"

Eachna looked furious. "Can't you control your horse?" she hissed.

"He n-never acts like this," Merida stuttered.

Eachna was still glaring when Fergus reappeared. "Lady Eachna, where did the boys go?" he asked.

"We were heading to the loch," Eachna said, "when Merida's horse went crazy!"

"Angus?" Fergus glanced curiously at Merida.

"I don't know what got into him," Merida said.

"That horse ran off with your sons," Eachna continued. "Maybe you should keep him away from your children. A horse with a mind of his own can be dangerous."

Merida gulped. She didn't think Angus was dangerous. But she also couldn't understand why he'd been acting so strange all morning. Or why he would run off without her.

"I just wanted to help!" Eachna cried. Then she sniffled and wiped her eyes, which surprised Merida. She hadn't realized Eachna's feelings were hurt so badly.

"I'm sorry that some members of my family were rude to you," Fergus said, "but I do appreciate your offer of help."

Eachna was sobbing now. Fergus looked panicked. He had no idea what to do.

Merida bit her lip. Mum wanted her to watch out for the triplets, and she'd done a terrible job. Plus, Mum always said a princess should be gracious—and the way she'd treated Eachna certainly wasn't polite. Whatever reservations Merida had, Eachna hadn't done anything wrong. If she got angry too easily when the triplets didn't listen, she'd hardly be the first adult to react that way.

Merida knew that Mum would want her to make Eachna feel welcome. So she took a deep breath and said, "I'm sorry, too, Lady Eachna. I know you were trying to help us. Will you give us another chance?"

Eachna raised her head. "What do you mean, another chance?"

"Will you join us for dinner tonight?" Merida asked.

Fergus's face lit up. "A fine idea, Merida!"

Eachna considered for a moment. Then she nodded. "Thank you, Princess Merida," she said. "I'd be honored to join you, your father, and your brothers for a meal tonight."

"Great," Fergus said. "Come back this evening and we'll show you a Clan DunBroch feast!"

"I can hardly wait," Eachna said, laughing.

Merida wondered why that laughter made her feel worse, not better.

Despite her excitement over the dinner invitation, Eachna was reluctant to leave. "Someone should go check on the boys. I could—"

"No, no, no," Fergus interrupted, "we'll take care of it. Thank you for everything, Lady Eachna, but we have a meal to prepare." He ushered her toward the path. "We'll see you this evening."

There was nothing Eachna could do but leave. Merida and Fergus waved good-bye until she was out of sight. Then Dad said, "Mum would be proud of you."

Merida tried to smile, but she couldn't shake the feeling that something was strange about Lady Eachna. She changed the subject. "I'm going to find Angus and the boys, Dad," she said. "It's my horse who ran off with them, so it's my responsibility to fix this."

Fergus nodded. "You're a good lass, Merida." He chuckled. "If they're still muddy, you'll have to get them clean, you know."

Merida groaned.

Angus had headed for the woods, so Merida

decided to start her search there. It was an
excellent guess—it didn't take long for her to
find Angus and the triplets.

Angus had brought the boys to a stream.
The four of them had clearly been playing in
the water. All the mud had washed off. When
Merida found them, they were wet but clean.

"At least you got rid of all that mud," she

muttered. The triplets spun around at the sound of her voice. When they saw their sister, they grinned.

"What would Mum say if she knew how you treated our guest?" Merida asked. She gave the boys a stern look.

They shrugged in response.

"Well, she wouldn't be happy. And she'd probably blame me for not keeping a good enough eye on you!" Merida said. "And in case you're wondering, Eachna was very upset that you ran off."

At just the mention of Eachna's name, her brothers' expressions changed. Hubert pretended to gag. Hamish stuck his tongue out. And Harris rolled his eyes.

"You don't like her, huh, boys?" Merida said.

The triplets shook their heads.

"Well, I invited her to dinner, so you're going to have to fake it."

That news was met by three identical eye rolls.

Merida went over to Angus and motioned for the boys to mount the horse. Then she got face to face with her friend. "I know this has been a strange trip so far. But whatever has gotten into you since we arrived here has to stop."

Angus tossed his head from side to side. Merida pulled herself onto his back. "Let's go home, boys."

Back at the cabin, Fergus was happy to see that everyone was safe—and clean. "We have a dinner party to plan," he said. "I suppose we should start with the food." He stroked his beard. "You know, I don't think I've ever planned a menu before. Elinor and Maudie usually take care of things like that."

"Mum left me in charge," Merida said, "and I think we should serve fish. Let's go fishing, Dad!"

Fergus clapped his hands. "Perfect! Go get your bow, and I'll get the fishing rods."

Merida nodded and hurried to get her bow and quiver. When she returned, Fergus had his fishing rod—but so did the triplets.

"Couldn't we go fishing alone, Dad?"

"I'm sorry," Fergus replied, "but I can't leave these little devils unsupervised. Look at what happened while we were talking to Eachna." He patted Merida's shoulder. "I think it's best if we all stay together."

Merida bit her lip. Fergus was already fixing the boys' fishing lines. He had his mind made up. She sighed. "Actually, Dad," she said, "the four of you can handle fishing. I'm going to gather some flowers to decorate the table."

"Are you sure, lass?" Fergus asked. "I'd like to have you with us."

Merida shook her head. "Next time, Dad."

She went to Angus and patted his nose. "You and I will ride into the forest to get flowers. That'll be fun."

Angus neighed and took a step backward.

"What's the matter?" Merida asked.

Angus stared at Merida for a moment, then

followed the triplets as they headed to the loch.

Merida couldn't believe it! Even her best friend wanted to be with the boys!

This was supposed to be a fun holiday. Merida had hoped to spend time alone with her parents, without those wee devils. But ever since Mum had left, Fergus was focused on the boys or on their new neighbor, Eachna. Even Angus seemed to prefer the company of the triplets.

Merida walked toward the woods. She needed to clear her head.

When the blue lights appeared, Merida wasn't expecting them.

"Will o' the wisps!" she gasped. In the past, the wisps had led her to good things. They had

also led her to trouble. But no matter what, they always led Merida to her fate.

At first, the trail of wisps took Merida deeper into the woods—or so she thought. The lands around the cabin were not as familiar to her as the highlands near Castle DunBroch. She followed the wisps faithfully, and soon she found herself on top of a hill. The wisps continued down the slope. Merida paused to look at where they were going.

The trail of wisps led directly to the spot where her family was fishing.

Merida's fists clenched. Her fate was her brothers. There was no way to escape them, no matter how much she wanted to. She groaned, then made her way to the loch.

"Merida!" Fergus cried when he spotted her. "What happened to the flower picking?"

Merida shrugged. "I decided I should be with all of you," she said. Her brothers smiled and waved her closer. She sighed. Then she joined them on the shore, thinking, *I guess there are worse fates than this.*

Chapter
7

It took most of the afternoon to catch a fish that Fergus thought was worthy of his cooking skills. Once it was caught, he shooed his children away. "I don't need you underfoot!" he said.

The triplets decided this was a great opportunity for a nap. They plopped down in the hammock outside the cabin. Soon the boys were snoring up a symphony.

"That's not a bad idea," Merida whispered to Angus as she led him to the stable. She made sure her horse was comfortable, then went to her bed to nap for a bit.

Merida didn't wake until evening. The sky had already begun to darken. Eachna would arrive soon, so she yawned and forced herself to get out of bed.

It was a beautiful, clear night. Merida knew her family would be dining under the stars. And indeed, she found her father standing by the table that overlooked the loch. But even though she could hear the triplets' tummies rumbling from hunger, Fergus had not yet called them to dinner. He seemed to be moving in slow motion, as if under a spell.

"Does Dad know it's time to eat?" Merida whispered. Hubert and Hamish shrugged. Harris shook his head. Then all three boys hugged their bellies.

"I know, lads, I know," Merida murmured. "I'm hungry, too. You must have dreadful collywobbles." The boys nodded.

Merida glanced up at Fergus. He was completely absorbed in trying to set the table. She leaned down to the boys and whispered, "If you go inside the house, there are a few sweet rolls left over from earlier. Maybe that will help your bellyaches?"

Merida's brothers all lunged forward at once. But it was only to hug their sister fiercely.

"Aw, lads," Merida crooned, tousling their hair. "Go on inside and have your snack. I'll see if I can lend Dad a hand to get dinner ready."

Merida approached Fergus, about to offer her help. But Dad beat her to it.

"Merida!" Fergus shouted. "I need you, lass!" He scratched his head as he stared down at the disarray on the dinner table. "I don't know where anything goes. Your mother always takes care of dinner parties."

Merida grabbed a stack of plates. "I got it,

Dad." She placed the plates around the table, then added goblets and napkins at each setting. "Is the food ready?" she asked.

"Ah, yes!" Fergus said, grinning. "That fine pike from earlier has been roasted." As he spoke, he took the fish off the fire and placed it on a platter. He presented it to Merida. "What do you think?"

"You did well, Dad!" Merida said. She closed her eyes and inhaled the aroma of the roasted fish.

Suddenly, someone called, "Hello, everyone!" Merida spun around at the sound of Eachna's voice. Once again, she looked beautiful. Her long hair was elaborately braided, though the ends still dripped water. Her dress was a dark blue fabric dotted with small flecks of silver that matched her long silver necklace. Looking at Eachna's dress was like looking at the moonlit loch.

"Lady Eachna," Fergus said. "Right on time. We were just finishing our preparations." He gestured for her to come closer.

Merida noticed a leaf caught in Eachna's necklace. She reached out to grab it. But when her hand got close, Eachna slapped it away.

"Ow!" Merida yelped. "Why did you do that?"

"What were *you* trying to do?" Eachna demanded.

"I saw something caught on your necklace!" Merida answered. "It's a leaf. I was just trying to get it out for you!"

Eachna stepped back and reached up to her

neck. "I'm sorry," she said. "You just startled me."

"Children!" Fergus called for the boys. "Take your places, everyone. We're going to start the meal now."

The triplets ran to the table. Merida took her seat to the right of her father. The boys sat in their chairs to his left.

"My lady," Fergus drawled, "we are ready to serve your dinner." He bowed and pulled out a chair for Eachna. But the only empty chair was the one across from Fergus—and that belonged to Mum.

As Merida watched Eachna take Elinor's place at their family table, her fingers clenched the stem of her goblet. She didn't like Eachna sitting in Mum's chair. No one else seemed to be bothered, though, so Merida forced herself to relax. She took a few deep breaths.

"I cooked this myself," Fergus announced. He carried the platter that held the main course and placed it in front of Eachna. "It's an old family recipe," he said. He removed the cover from the platter.

As soon as he did that, Eachna's face went pale. "Is that"—she gulped—"is that a *fish?*" She practically spat the last word.

"It's a pike," Fergus explained, flustered. "We caught it earlier and—"

Eachna cut him off. "I don't eat fish."

Fergus opened and closed his mouth, but nothing came out. The triplets stared intently at their plates. Merida could feel anger bubbling inside her. She had felt bad earlier about hurting Eachna's feelings. But now it was clear that

Eachna wasn't very nice herself. Dad had worked so hard on this meal, and she was making him feel like a failure.

"I think pike is delicious," Merida said. Eachna couldn't sit in Mum's seat and treat her family like this. Merida wouldn't let her be mean to Dad without doing something about it. She helped herself to some pike and served some to the boys. Then, glaring, she turned to Eachna. "You live on the banks of a loch and you don't eat fish?"

"I don't care for the taste," Eachna snapped.

Merida had had enough of this rude behavior. She opened her mouth to tell Eachna to leave. But before she could say anything, the meal was interrupted.

"Look!" Fergus said, pointing off into the

distance. "Someone's coming!"

Everyone at the table turned to see what he was pointing at. It was another rider, wearing MacGuffin colors.

Merida's heart raced. The rider must have word from Mum!

She rose from her seat so quickly that she knocked over her goblet. But she didn't even look back. She and her father went straight to the unexpected guest and helped him dismount.

"Your Majesty," the rider said.

"Yes, yes, no need for formalities," Fergus said. "Do you have a message from my wife?"

The man nodded. "Queen Elinor sent me on ahead to tell you she will be back at your royal cabin tomorrow."

"Ah, that's wonderful news!" Fergus

bellowed. Merida clapped her hands and cheered. The triplets jumped onto their seats and started dancing a jig. Fergus and Merida joined in until Fergus scooped up all his children in a great bear hug. "Your mother will be here tomorrow!"

When he let them go, Merida noticed Eachna's scowl. But as soon as Eachna's eyes met Fergus's, the scowl changed to a smile.

"I'm so happy for you, King Fergus," she said.

Merida raised an eyebrow. Eachna hadn't *looked* happy.

"Thank you, Lady Eachna," Fergus replied. "We miss Elinor very much. And now we have a lot to do before she arrives!"

Once again, Eachna's face changed. This time, the smile melted into a smirk. "Let me help you, King Fergus. I'll take your sons for a ride in my rowboat so you and Princess Merida can do what you need to do."

After the way Eachna had acted before the meal started, there was no way Merida was going to let her near her little brothers. She opened her mouth to object. But Fergus beat her to it.

"I appreciate the offer," he said, "but tonight we're going to work together as a family."

Eachna nodded and pushed away from the table. "I understand. I'll stop by tomorrow to see if you need help then." She waved good-bye, but Merida and her brothers were too busy celebrating to wave back.

Not that Merida would have wanted to wave anyway.

Chapter
8

"Merida! Boys!" Fergus called. "Wake up!"

Merida frowned and tried to bury herself deeper under the blankets. "It's not even sunrise yet," she groaned. But Dad wouldn't give up.

"Come on, children," he said. He tugged at her blanket with one hand and the blanket over the triplets with the other. "It's a fine morning!

Your mum will be back today, so we need to get this place cleaned up."

The boys glowered and lunged for their blanket. But Dad pulled it out of the way. He pointed to a stack of mops, brooms, and cleaning brushes. "Go make yourselves useful!"

Merida moaned, but she forced herself to get up. After all, they were cleaning for Mum, and Merida couldn't wait to see her.

It took a while, but finally, Dad deemed the cabin acceptable. Yet by late afternoon there was still no sign of Mum.

"What do we do now?" Merida asked.

The triplets pointed to the platter of cakes Dad had set out on the table. They grinned from ear to ear. It was clear they wanted to eat. As usual.

Fergus sighed. "Go ahead, lads. Just try to leave a few for your mother." The boys started devouring the cakes like animals. Fergus looked at Merida. "Are you hungry, too?"

Even if Merida had wanted a cake or two, her brothers were practically slobbering all over them. She shook her head. "I'm going to take Angus for a ride. Maybe I can catch some fish for us to cook for Mum tonight."

"That sounds lovely," Fergus said. "You catch them, and I'll cook them. Elinor will be so impressed!"

Merida grabbed her bow and quiver and went to the stable. As she saddled Angus, she said, "I'm happy Mum will be home soon. Maybe then Eachna won't need to 'help' again."

Angus neighed.

"You've never liked her, have you, boy?" Merida whispered. "I'm not sure why *you* feel that way, but I think I share the feeling."

Merida and Angus rode out and headed toward the loch. It was as if Angus could read Merida's mind—as soon as they got into the open, he changed from a trot to a full-on gallop. The wind whipped through Merida's hair as she and her best friend raced around the loch.

When Angus finally stopped in a clearing on the far side of the loch, Merida felt happier than she had since Mum had left. She leaped from the saddle and patted Angus's nose. "Thank you, Angus," she whispered. "I needed that."

Merida left Angus to graze and went to the bank. She peered into the water. The loch was crystal clear. She could see several fat fish

swimming lazily in the shallows. She drew her bow and prepared to hunt.

"What are you doing?"

The voice startled Merida, and her arrow went astray. It landed in the mud, far from the fish.

She turned to see who had spoken. "Eachna!" she cried. "Where did you come from?"

Eachna smiled that same cold smile Merida was getting used to seeing. "I was out for a walk and I saw you. What are you doing here with your bow?"

Merida's eyes narrowed. "I'm hunting for fish to cook for Mum. As you know, she's coming back today." She couldn't be sure, but Eachna seemed angry. Not that Merida cared. She looked back to the water and drew her bow again. "We won't need you to stop by the cabin anymore," she hissed under her breath.

"How nice for you," Eachna drawled. "But wouldn't your mother prefer fresh venison? Or a nice pheasant?"

"We have venison and pheasant all the time at home," Merida answered. "I think she'd love a fresh fish from the loch." She giggled. "I know you don't care for the taste, Lady Eachna, but my mother and I can't get enough!"

Merida spied a slow-moving fish and took aim with her bow. But right before her eyes, the clear loch water roiled and became cloudy. In a moment, all the fish were hidden from sight.

"What?" Merida cried. "I've never seen that

happen! There's not even any wind." She stared at Eachna. "The water just turned murky for no reason!"

"Maybe it's a sign that you shouldn't be fishing," Eachna suggested.

Merida glared at Eachna's back as she walked away. Then she shook her head and glanced at the water again. It was still cloudy.

Angus was grazing happily, so Merida decided to walk by herself along the edge of the loch. Maybe she could find a better spot to hunt. But no matter where she looked, the water didn't seem to be any clearer.

"I guess there'll be no fish today." Merida sighed. She slung her bow over her shoulder and got ready to go back to Angus.

That was when she saw the white horse

again. *How did she get here?* Merida wondered. She hadn't noticed anyone or anything around her since Eachna left.

The horse trotted closer, and then stopped on the bank of the loch. She tossed her head as if calling directly to Merida. Merida felt a sudden urge to ride the white horse. She slowly walked toward her.

The sound of hoofbeats distracted her for a

moment. She wondered if it was Angus coming to find her. But it didn't matter. All she could think about was the white horse.

Suddenly, Angus appeared between Merida and the other horse. He neighed and stomped his feet. But Merida kept trying to reach the white horse. Somewhere in the back of her mind, she knew she really didn't want to. But the horse was so beautiful she couldn't help herself.

Angus's nostrils flared as Merida pushed past him. He nudged her with his head, but she couldn't look at him. The white horse had taken a few steps back—Merida was afraid she'd leave if she didn't hurry.

Angus gave up on Merida. Instead, he cantered toward the white horse. At first, he just seemed curious. But when he got close enough, he rammed his head into the horse's flank.

The white horse staggered back. Her green eyes showed fear and surprise.

Angus pawed at the ground and lowered his head as if to ram her again. But the white horse didn't give him the chance. She turned and galloped away.

Merida blinked. Her head felt fuzzy. Angus had come over to her and was nuzzling her cheek.

"Oh, hi, Angus. I don't know what got into me," Merida whispered. She shook her head to clear it. She didn't know why, but she had the feeling that Angus had just saved her from something.

Chapter 9

Merida arrived at the cabin exhausted. She hardly remembered the ride home. She had trusted Angus to get her back safely, and he did.

As soon as Fergus saw his daughter, he bounded over to her and lifted her out of the saddle. "Did you catch a fish, lass?" he asked.

Merida shook her head. "No, Dad. The water

was too murky. I couldn't see any fish to hunt."

Fergus scratched his head. "That's odd. The loch is usually so clear."

"I know," Merida said. "It was all very strange."

"Sometimes that happens at this loch," someone said from behind them.

"Lady Eachna!" Fergus cried. "We weren't expecting you."

Merida felt the heat rising in her face as soon as she heard Eachna's name. She spun around to face the woman and tried to keep from scowling.

"I brought you some vegetables from my garden," Eachna said. "I thought you could cook something for your wife's homecoming. And I wanted to see if you needed any help today."

Why is she always offering to help? Merida

thought. She didn't want Eachna here, and she knew Angus didn't either.

Yet Merida was still surprised when, without warning, Angus lunged forward and almost pushed Eachna to the ground. The vegetables fell out of her hands and scattered everywhere.

"Angus!" Merida shouted, grabbing for his bridle.

"That horse is too jittery," Fergus said. "Did something happen earlier?"

Merida started to shake her head. But then she stopped. "There was something," she said. "There was this other horse—"

Eachna cut Merida off. "Another horse from hours ago doesn't explain a horse acting like this now," she snapped. "You should lock him in the stable."

"That sounds like a good idea, Merida," Fergus suggested.

Merida gave Eachna a dark look. "Maybe he's just hungry. We did ride a long way." She led Angus to the trough. "Have some food, boy," she crooned. "I filled it for you with sweet, fresh hay earlier. Eat and calm down."

Angus yanked his head away from the trough so hard that Merida was caught off balance. She stumbled and almost fell to the ground.

"Angus!" Fergus barked. "What has gotten into you, boy?" He turned to Merida. "Tether that horse out in the woods behind the cabin. His temper is all out of sorts."

Fergus was usually the easygoing parent. He was quick to forgive and slow to punish. He let the triplets get away with countless pranks, and he even covered for Merida with Mum at times when she did something particularly un-princess-like. But right now, Merida didn't see any good humor in her father. He looked downright angry, so Merida simply nodded. As she threw a halter over Angus's neck, she overheard Fergus apologizing to Eachna.

Angus glared at Eachna. When Merida tried to lead him away, he refused to move.

"Angus, please just come with me," Merida

begged. But her horse fought her. He pulled at the lead rope until it snapped. Merida couldn't remember ever seeing Angus so unruly.

Though he had been bred to be a war horse, he'd never shown an inclination for aggression. Still, he was a Clydesdale, strong and powerful. Merida wasn't strong enough to hold him back by herself.

But Fergus, the Bear King, was. He grabbed Angus's bridle and stared right in his eyes. "You might be able to fight that little lass, but you will go where I tell you to go."

Fergus forcefully dragged Angus away. Merida followed. She hated seeing Angus so distressed. She wanted to soothe him, but every time she tried to get close, Fergus cautiously pushed her back.

"Careful, Merida," he ordered. "There's something wrong with this horse. I don't want you to get hurt."

Fergus managed to wrench Angus back into the woods, but it took a great deal of effort. When he tried to tie Angus to a tree, the horse bucked and sent Fergus sprawling.

"Angus, please!" Merida begged. "Why are you acting this way?"

Fergus got up almost immediately and lunged for Angus's bridle. But before he could reach it, Angus nudged Merida with his nose so hard it turned her around. That was when she saw Eachna leading her brothers away from the cabin.

"Harris!" Merida screamed. "Hubert! Hamish! Where are you going?"

The boys glanced over their shoulders at her. But their expressions were blank, just as they had been the first night at the loch when they had followed the white horse.

"Come on, lads," Eachna crooned. "We're almost there."

The triplets moved even closer to Eachna and kept following her without hesitation.

"What has she done to them?" Merida cried.

Angus's ears were pinned back close to his neck and he pawed at the ground. Fergus had a firm hold on the bridle so Angus couldn't run away. But the sound that came out of Angus was more like a roar than anything else. Eachna heard it and turned around. Her eyes met Merida's.

Suddenly, Merida realized something. "Her

eyes!" she gasped. "She has the same eyes as the mysterious white horse! She's a kelpie!"

"What are you saying, Merida?" Fergus asked.

"Look at her, Dad!" Merida shouted. "Her hair is always wet. She doesn't eat fish. And her eyes!"

Fergus looked directly at Eachna. Almost instantly, his jaw dropped. "Jings crivens help ma boab! Eachna is a kelpie! And she has my sons!"

Chapter
10

Fergus loosened his hold on Angus's bridle. Immediately, Merida leaped onto her horse's back. "Hurry! We have to get to them!"

Angus galloped off while Fergus ran behind them. "Don't wait for me!" Fergus bellowed. "Save the lads!"

Soon Angus and Merida reached the cabin.

At the pace Angus was moving, they'd reach the boys in just a few heartbeats. Merida leaned forward and urged her horse to go even faster. "We can't let them get to the water!" she shrieked.

Angus snorted and galloped like the wind. Eachna saw him approaching and scowled. Then she raised her arms and gazed at Angus's trough of water. It stood between her and Merida. Her eyes blazed with an eerie green light, and a moment later, the water took on a shape of its own. Before Merida's eyes, the water became three stomping, kicking horses. And they were blocking the path to the triplets.

One of the watery horses reared up. Then all three charged Angus.

"Ach! Where is my bow?" Merida cried. She had nothing with her to use against this magic— no bow, no sword, not even a staff or a rock. But she could hear great, lumbering footsteps approaching. It was her father, catching up.

"Dad!" she screamed. "Help us!"

Fergus saw the watery horses about to attack his daughter. With a roar, he drew his great sword and rushed to protect her. "Merida, get the boys!" he yelled.

Fergus swung at one of the watery horses and it disappeared into a puddle of water. "This magic is no match for me. Go save my sons!"

Merida was worried for her father's safety, but she forced herself to concentrate on Eachna. Angus galloped toward the triplets.

Eachna had seen how Fergus had already

defeated one of the watery horses. Her eyes
began to glow once again, but this time, no
horses appeared out of the water. Rather,
Eachna herself shape-shifted into the now-
familiar white horse. The enchanted boys
climbed onto her back, and she raced to the
water's edge.

Merida's eyes narrowed. As a horse, Eachna
could move much faster. But there was no way

she was faster than Angus. "That scaffy kelpie chose the wrong horse to race," Merida hissed. "Come on, Angus!"

Angus neighed and seemed to double his speed. In just a few moments, he was neck and neck with Eachna. He leaned over to bite at her. Merida strained to hold on as the two horses struggled.

Then Eachna reared up on her hind legs and began to pound at Angus with her hooves. Merida screamed and tried to shield herself with her arms. But Angus pulled back enough for Merida to be out of range of Eachna's hooves. Then he followed suit and reared up himself.

In the ruckus, the triplets were thrown from Eachna's back, and Merida was thrown from Angus's. "Boys!" Merida hollered. "Come to me!"

But the triplets still appeared to be enchanted. They stood motionless, staring at Eachna.

Merida ran to her brothers and tried to yank them away to safety. "Harris! Hubert! Hamish!" she shrieked. "We need to go!"

The boys looked at her blankly. They didn't move.

"Please, boys, please come with me," she begged. "I'll give you my dessert for a year. Five years! Just come with me now!"

The triplets didn't even blink. They must have been under some sort of spell.

Merida turned to the horses. They were still battling each other on their hind legs. Angus's mane bristled and his hooves cracked against Eachna's. Then Eachna landed a blow to Angus's head that sent him reeling backward.

"Angus! No!" Merida cringed as Angus staggered.

Eachna was headed toward Angus, ready to strike again. Merida ran to Eachna and grabbed for the silver bridle around her neck.

"You leave him alone!" Merida cried. The bridle slipped through her fingers as Eachna raised her head. Merida pounded on Eachna's flank with her fists, but that didn't slow the horse down. The white horse spun around to face Merida, ready to attack.

But before Eachna could land a blow, Angus leaped in and grasped Eachna's bridle between his teeth. As soon as he did so, Eachna stopped pursuing Merida. She strained against Angus's hold on her, but she didn't attack.

The bridle! Merida realized that Eachna's

bridle must have magical powers. Perhaps even enough to control the kelpie. She rushed into the fray and clawed at the bridle. "Angus!" she shouted. "Don't let go!"

Angus snorted. His teeth remained clenched on the bit of the bridle he'd managed to grasp. Out of the corner of her eye, Merida saw the triplets' faces begin to change. The boys blinked and shook their heads as if they were trying to wake up. She locked eyes with Angus and yelled, "Her powers are weakened when we hold on to her bridle!"

When Merida said that, Eachna's eyes widened and she appeared to be afraid. Merida knew she'd guessed correctly. She tightened her hands on the silvery straps as much as she could.

The kelpie made one last desperate attempt

to get free of Merida's and Angus's grasps. She turned her eyes to the loch and they began to glow again. Merida looked over her shoulder to see what Eachna was doing. What she saw made her heart sink.

The water at the edge of the loch seemed to come to life just as the water in the trough had done near the cabin. But this time, instead of watery horses, the magic created watery tentacles—and those tentacles were about to wrap around the boys.

Merida didn't want to let go of Eachna's bridle. But she couldn't let her brothers be harmed. She had no choice. She unclenched her fingers and ran toward the triplets. Before the watery tentacles reached them, Merida pulled the triplets away.

As soon as Merida let go of the bridle, Eachna saw her chance. Angus couldn't hold on by himself, so she pulled away from him. Merida bit her lip and wrapped her arms around the triplets to protect them from Eachna's next move. But instead of attacking again, the kelpie retreated. She galloped away across the loch and seemed to disappear into the water. When she was out of sight, the watery tentacles dissolved into harmless puddles on the ground.

Merida and the boys watched Eachna disappear, but they were frozen in place. When Angus came over, they moved—but only to wrap their arms around him. "Thank you, boy," Merida whispered, patting his nose and then kissing it. "I'm sorry we didn't understand what you were trying to warn us about."

They stood embracing until a voice brought them back to reality.

"What happened to all of you?" Elinor stared wide-eyed at her soaked family.

"Mum!" Merida ran to her mother, the triplets on her heels. All four children hugged Elinor fiercely. A moment later, Fergus joined them, enveloping his family in a bear hug.

"You're all wet!" Elinor cried. "And you're getting me wet! What's going on here?"

"It was a kelpie!" Merida exclaimed. "She tried to take the triplets!"

"A kelpie?" Queen Elinor whipped her head around to look at her husband. "Fergus, what is she talking about?"

King Fergus nodded somberly. "It's true, Elinor. There was a kelpie in the loch. And she did her best to take our lads."

Elinor's jaw dropped. "But kelpies aren't real!" she cried.

Merida rolled her eyes. "Even after everything this family has been through, Mum still doesn't believe in kelpies."

Elinor sighed. "I deserved that," she admitted. "So, what happened? How did you two battle a kelpie?"

Fergus smiled. "Merida did it. Our daughter protected our lads. She's the reason we're all safe. And I'm very proud of her."

Merida blushed. "Thank you, Dad." Then she pulled Angus forward. "But I don't deserve all the credit. I couldn't have done it without Angus!"

Elinor patted Angus's muzzle, then put an arm around Merida. "I'm proud of you both. I knew I could trust you to be in charge!"

"Thank you, Mum." Merida laughed. "But please don't do it again anytime soon!

Ula Blocksage

Sudipta Bardhan-Quallen is the author of more than forty books for children, including *Duck, Duck, Moose!*; *Tyrannosaurus Wrecks!*; and *Orangutangled*. Her books have been named to the California Readers Collection, the Junior Library Guild, the Bank Street Best Children's Books of the Year Lists, and the Amelia Bloomer Book List. She lives outside Philadelphia with her family and an imaginary pony named Penny. Visit her at sudipta.com.

EVERY PRINCESS HAS A STORY.
EVERY STORY HAS A BEGINNING.

COMING SOON!

A NEW CHAPTER BOOK SERIES:
DISNEY PRINCESS BEGINNINGS

Young Belle is happy at home with her father the inventor. But at school she feels like an outsider. Then she discovers a run-down bookshop in the village. Can she get her classmates to see how wonderful books are—and save the bookstore from closing?

EVERY PRINCESS HAS A STORY.
EVERY STORY HAS A BEGINNING.

COMING SOON!

A NEW CHAPTER BOOK SERIES:

DISNEY PRINCESS BEGINNINGS

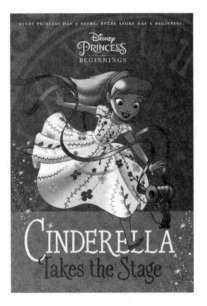

Young Ella, or "Cinderella," as her parents fondly call her, has always dreamed of winning the Midsummer Festival's puppet contest. But then she meets Val, who has the very same dream. Will Ella be the best puppeteer—or the best friend?